THE TEENAGER

by *Ure Ude*

The Teenager by *Ure Ude*

This book is written to provide information and motivation to readers. Its purpose is not to render any type of psychological, legal, or professional advice of any kind. The content is the sole opinion and expression of the author, and not necessarily that of the publisher.

Printed in the United States of America.

ISBN 978-1-949746-06-8 (Paperback)
ISBN 978-1-949746-07-5 (Digital)

Lettra Press books may be ordered through booksellers or by contacting:

Lettra Press LLC
18229 E 52nd Ave.
Denver City, CO 80249
1 303 586 1431 | info@lettrapress.com
www.lettrapress.com

Contents

Dedication

This book is dedicated to everyone that will read it, to children, to teachers, to parents, and to my family. I would like to thank my mother who loves to see a child read, and my father who was the best dad anyone could have.

Acknowledgments

I thank my husband and children. Living with them, made the writing of this book come naturally. I thank my friends:

In addition, I'd like to thank Dr. Brij Mansi for proofreading the book. Dr. Mansi has her Ph.D. in English. Also, Dr. Mansi is a teacher.

Finally, to the young people, who will see themselves in the characters of this book. Read on!

Introduction

This book is for young people, parents, teachers, guardians or adults. You will relive your lives with your young ones in this book. It is entertaining, educational and it is worth your while to read.

About the Author

Ure Ude is a wife, a mother of four and has worked with young people of various ages in the school system.

Mrs. ***Ude*** earned her bachelor's degree from Howard University. She worked for an oil company from where she retired.

She has interest in the welfare of young people, no wonder she is also a foster parent.

Chapter One

The Couple

Mr. Johnny Linden and his wife lived in a remote village, situated between the East and the West.

They had a lovely son called Morris. Morris was such a fine young lad, that the Lindens swore to bring him up in the best of morals.

Their desire was that Morris would grow up to be an example to his peers or other young people like him and this is the desire of every parent.

The Lindens, in order to fulfill their desire of raising Morris to be the best, were very calculated in what they did or said around Morris because children learn by example.

As Morris grew up, he became inquisitive about life. (He would ask questions). He asked his parents where the sun lives.

The Lindens would answer, "The sun lives in the East but goes to the West to sleep."

Sometimes when his Mom wore pants, Morris would say, "Mom, you are a boy today, I can see you are wearing your pants." These questions amused the parents. The Mom would reply, "Oh, so what I wear determines my gender?"

Chapter Two

The Parents Groom Morris with the Help of Good Books

Morris grew up handsome, innocent and naive about life. The mother and father set out one weekend and bought books on the anatomy of the human body and reproduction.

Morris read all the books and when asked by his parents, about the books, Morris jumped with excitement and said, "Babies come from human reproductive organs, not delivered at night by God."

Mr. and Mrs. Linden were so happy and relieved that Morris learnt a lesson on reproduction, a topic that is not easy to introduce to a child.

Mrs. Linden, talking to her husband, said, "Remember Dear, your niece Jane is gonna have a baby, and it is great that our son Morris read those books to learn more about life.

Mr. Linden thought the books worked like a miracle. Books take you to places and teaches you what you do not know.

Chapter Three

Morris Learns Values of a Good Society

Mrs. Linden said, "Son, now that you know that babies come from human embryos, it is a good idea to discuss values of a good society."

The father said, "Yes son, we all love children and society prefers that you grow up and get married before getting a child and that is at least after age 18, and maybe even above."

Morris said, "Why 18 and above?" Some girl got a baby, but she was not eighteen. The mother said, "This is because before age 18, children are not yet adults. Any teen having a child before the age 18 means a kid raising another kid. Morris, you know, raising a child is sure not easy."

Here are the responsibilities of a new Mom and Dad:

The baby must have a good home, a good job for the father to take care of the rent, milk, diapers, clothes, food, and a car for mobility. There ought to be health insurance, etc. The young parents must stay awake at night as the baby needs attention. They have to clean diapers every time the baby goes or eases itself. (You know what).

Morris cut in, "Mom, please, I don't think I want to have a baby for a long long time. I don't ever want to clean anyone else. Can we end this discussion Mom and Dad?"

The father laughed and said, "Morris we don't mean to scare you, but this is the reality of life situations. You see, you have to know these things. Morris said, "Mom and Dad have we finished our discussion?"

Chapter Four

Morris Learns About Deadly Mistakes

Mom said, "Morris, do you know there are mistakes that people learn from, and mistakes that end peoples' lives? This is why we don't want to have you ignorant."

"Oh my," Morris exclaimed, "are there mistakes that kill?

"Oh yeah!" said Dad. "Son if you engage in a fight and get wounded, your wound might heal, and you will probably learn not to fight again, knowing that you could be wounded in a fight. Or, if you do not study or do not do your home work, that can cause you to fail your exams. You could learn to study and do your home work in order to pass your exams."

Dad continued, "Have you ever heard of AIDS?" Morris replied, "What is that?" "I have heard of it and I learned it kills many people in many places, like Africa and maybe Asia."

Mr. Linden said, "Not only in Africa, but in London, Europe, America and many parts of the world. This is not the disease you get from dirty places. This is the kind you get from having fun-sleeping around.

"This is why children are advised not to engage in casual sex. That means wait until you are married before you have sex. When you are married, only keep to your wife or husband and then you will not have to worry about contracting AIDS, STDs, or other venereal diseases. If you are married and play around on your husband or wife, then you may contract these diseases.

It is better to abstain from casual sex than to make a grave mistake.

"This is not to blame anyone that made that kind of mistake. Some use what they call condoms for protection. Some condoms are not really protecting you. They have holes in them and some pop open.

"The other day, I listened to a teenage symposium and I learned that some condoms have microscopic holes. This makes them unsafe and may not protect people from contracting the AIDS virus. This means you cannot see the holes with your eyes, and you will think you have protection when you actually don't."

"Oh my goodness!" Morris said, "this is scary. Thank you Mom and Dad. It is good to know the mistakes you die from. I am not ready to kill myself just for a stupid thing they call sex. Yak! The other day my friends were talking about that kind of girl friend stuff. Someone like Mandy thought that was cool. I am glad I know this – I'll tell them."

Chapter Five

Morris Learns Etiquette and Good Manners

Morris grew bigger and more handsome. One day Morris was to go out with Mom while Dad sat in the living room watching both mother and son.

Morris rushed out of the door as his mother walked behind him. He didn't hold the door open and his Mom struggled to hold the door as the door came smashing in her face. His father roared, "Morris you need to come back here." He came back as urgently as his Dad's call warranted.

Dad continues, "Morris, you need to hold the door open for ladies. You shut the door on my wife and your Mom. You just ran out of the house and sort of shut the door in her face. Remember this is my lady and your Mom."

Morris apologized saying, "I am sorry Dad. I will learn to hold the door open for Mom and other ladies." Dad said, "well done." "Well done son!"

Mrs. Linden yawned, covering her mouth like a lady. Shortly after that, Morris yawned with a very wide open mouth with a shout e-e-h.

Mrs. Linden said, "Morris you have to learn to cover your mouth when you yawn. You don't just open your mouth wide like that without covering it." Morris rolled his eyes and said, "I have learned that too." At dinner, Morris was sneezing indiscriminately and almost spat all over the food.

Mrs. Linden said, "Morris if you breathe in when you feel the urge to sneeze you will control how you sneeze. Or you can just cover your mouth. Morris was surprised that he could control his sneezing that way, and he again thanked his Mom for teaching him another lesson on etiquette and good manners.

Mrs. Linden also taught her son to greet his teachers at school by saying "Good morning Madam or Sir."

Mrs. Linden said, "Morris do you know that we have two ears, but we can not hear two people talking at the same time?"

This happened while Dad was talking and Morris started talking too.

Morris thanked Mom, and said, "I will always wait my turn to speak even in school. My teacher said the same thing the other day." "Oh great, I'm glad to hear that," Mom said.

Chapter Six

The Symposium by the Kids Lovers Association

Mrs. Linden brought out two tickets from her pocket and said, "Morris, do you have two friends to go for a teenage symposium? A social worker friend of mine Mrs. Dave gave these tickets to me. It is taking place at the city hall down the road." "Oh yeah Mom!", Morris screamed. "My friend John and his sister will be glad to go." John and Nancy were two kids who lived happily with their foster parents. Morris asked, "when is it taking place?" Mom said, "tomorrow at 4:00 p.m."

Morris went to bed excited. The following day, he woke up ready to inform his friends of the free tickets to the symposium. At a little before 4:00 p.m., the trio were at the symposium eating popcorn and sipping soft drinks all free from the organizers. The hall was packed full with young people all excited to be a part of the action.

The stage opened with Jim Donald, a student with a microphone. Jim is a very lively and outgoing boy. He is a fun and likeable person. Jim said, "Let's welcome Mrs. Scott." Mrs Scott showed up on stage as the curtain opened. The students chanted, "Yeah!."

She collected the microphone and said "Welcome wonderful young people. How are you enjoying your refreshments?" They went "yeah" again. "This is courtesy of The Kids Lovers Association." The students cheered and chanted, "yeah!" and some whistled to show their excitement, and approval.

"Mr. George, the principal of Jet School will take up the stage to speak on Etiquette and Good Manners in School (EAGMIS) which is the topic of today's symposium, as you can see from your tickets and flyers," Mrs. Scott announced.

Mr. George elegantly mounted the stage the way almost everyone knew he must be in great physical health for a man his age about mid 50s.

Mr. George said, "I welcome you to this special occasion, and I want to introduce the members of the Kids Lovers Association to you. Most of them are teachers, parents, government workers and business people.

"They have one thing in common - love for the future generation." The kids cheered, "yeah!" He continued, "Today is a special day in the hearts of the members of the Kids Lovers Association, because their dreams have come true.

"It is the first of many events to come. Honorable and dearly beloved members, please come up on stage." They all trooped up the stage, smiling. The auditorium roared with cheers, because many children saw their teachers, parents, aunts, uncles, and neighbors etc. As they vacated the stage, Mr. George introduced Mr. Blake to take the stage. "He is the master of ceremony for today," as Mr. Blake appeared, the students, yelled out, "MC, MC!" And some whistled while the rest of them cheered, "yeah!"

Mr. Blake came out trying to suppress a wild laugh "ha ha young people, when we tell you we are kids lovers, believe it! We know what you like. Listen to this, "neighborhood musicians show up," he announced. The curtain opened and music boomed from the neighborhood musicians singing, "Who Let the Dogs Out?", Who? Who? Who? Who? Who let the dogs out? Who? Who? Who? Who?!"

The auditorium went wild with the students dancing. The music went on for some ten minutes of dancing, jumping and fun. Mr. Blake the MC said, "Mr. George once again," Mr. George came back in his usual elegant manner on stage, collecting the microphone from Mr. Blake and said, "Hey isn't that great?" The young people screamed, "yeah." Mr. George said, "I told you that you would love it today!" The young crowd said, "yeah!" Most of the young people were still dancing even after the music had stopped. This will show you the kind of energy in the auditorium.

Chapter Seven

The Symposium Teaches about Students Appearances on School Premises

Mr. George came on stage and said, "Calm down young people. Our program starts with a topic on Appearances on School Premises. I will tell you a short story.

Once there was a poster on an office wall that said, 'the way you dress, is the way you are perceived, and the way you are perceived, is the way you are treated.' After I read through the words of the poster, it did something to my mind, my spirit was awakened to be more attentive to the way I look.

The statement made so much sense to me. Imagine that you see a man along the road dressed in rags. Immediately an impression is created in your mind that this man is mentally disturbed, or he could be an alcoholic, or a drug addict.

In order to be treated with dignity and respect, one has to be in good or clean appearance. This means look clean around the school premises or any where for that matter. The following duties early in the morning will lead to a clean person or good personal hygiene.

1. Taking a bath with soap before coming to school will make you look clean,
2. Brushing the teeth with whatever dental cleaning agent available will make teeth clean,
3. Using mouth wash helps to keep the mouth clean, and also stops bad breath,
4. Applying cream to the body and the face with any lotion or Vaseline available,
5. Putting on washed under wears that way you smell clean,
6. Putting on washed clothes,
7. Putting on comfortable shoes and clean socks,
8. Having hair combed makes one look well groomed,
9. Having finger nails and toe nails clipped,
10. Appearing in the proper uniform in school where uniforms are required.

Any student approaching the school compound to attend classes is expected to be up to date in appearance. This does not mean expensive dresses or shoes. Sometimes cheap shoes fit just as well as expensive ones."

At the end of Mr. George's speech, two neat students came out to parade as an example of acceptable appearance. While two students with wrong appearance came with their attire to show inappropriate dress wear in schools.

The Symposium Teaches Students on Items that Should Be In A Student's Bag

Mr. George continued to say that most students carry book bags to school which contain the students belonging such as: books, writing materials or any other thing students might need to aid them in being productive in school.

He stressed that certain kinds of items that should not be in a students bag are guns, knives, and drugs.

He also explained that many students have been in the news lately for very serious misdemeanors, just because they brought the wrong things to school, and had to use them when they got angry.

He listed the following items which should not be in a students' book bag:

1. Any sharp objects such as knives, or sharp metals.
2. Any rifle such as a gun of any sort.
3. Any drugs or tablets except needed for survival and permission should be sought and such drugs should be left with the school nurse to administer.
4. No dangerous sprays.

Chapter Eight

The Symposium Teaches Good Behavior

Mr. George continued, and said, that "Behavior on school premises should be one of politeness."

He advised that there should be no usage of curse words in school, and that students should obey school rules, taking directions, not talking back or being rude, rather that they (students), should be gentle in their speaking and be respectful to school authorities. He said that a student should neither argue nor challenge the teachers, rather a student should be honest and truthful, upright, trust worthy, diligent, industrious, amorous, cautious, and ambitious.

He encouraged every student to come to class expecting respect from both, peers and school authorities; and that the only way to be respected and treated nicely is by starting to respect others. This is why it is said that respect is reciprocal. In other words, respect others to get respect from them, or, if I want respect, then let it begin with me.

On this note Mr. George handed the microphone back to the MC Mr. Blake for the next speaker Mrs. Scott, while the crowd cheered – yeah!

Chapter Nine

The Symposium Lectures Students to Be Calm In The Classroom

Mrs. Scott taking the microphone said, "We are going to talk about the behavior in our classrooms. Remember this is where we spend the greater part of our day.

A student should come to class ready to listen first, if the student needs to talk, he or she should do so by seeking permission signified by raising of a hand.

This is so because we have two ears, but unfortunately we cannot hear two people talk at the same time.

Most classrooms have students between 15 and 25 in numbers or even more. For this reason, self-control and a lot of cooperation is needed from students. Noise making is very rampant in our schools today. It is one teacher against 20 or more students. The most needed assistance by students to the teacher is that students should learn how to stay in a class without talking. There should be a calm atmosphere if there should be learning."

Now, let's believe there will be better behavior in our classrooms. "Thank you for being quiet."

Chapter Ten

The Symposium Teaches Young People

Good Behavior to the Teachers

Mr. Blake thanked Mrs. Scott and called Dr. Coral Moore to talk about behavior to the teachers. Dr. Coral Moore came on stage looking very well dressed. She started, "young people, I am pleased to be in your midst and happy for what is happening today and as usual we teachers are continuing to touch lives. I am here to talk to you about your behavior to your teachers. First and foremost, teachers are learned men and women who have mastered the art of imparting k nowledge from their diverse Fidelit y elds of study to students. They also mastered the art of holding students spellbound during lectures, and making learning fun.

Every successful person in all fields of endeavor, one way or another, was taught by a teacher. Teachers touch lives. Teachers mold lives at a very desperate time of need. They make lawyers, accountants, engineers, doctors, nurses and so on.

Students are encouraged to respect their teachers, as they respect their parents. It will be very unwise to disrespect someone who makes decisions about your progress in life. Teachers are usually elders to young people. So they deserve to be respected."Mr. Blake thanked Dr. Coral Moore, and handed the microphone to Mrs. Cathy Pendleton.

The Symposium Teaches on Good Behavior Toward Fellow Students.

Mrs. Cathy Pendleton spoke on behavior toward fellow students, while in school. She spoke to the young people and said, "You have each other at school to take care of. Be friendly and helpful to each other."

When a student is quiet in class that is being helpful, not only to the teacher and himself, but he or she is making the atmosphere conducive for learning for the other students. A student can be a caring person, a team player and a good listener. Without listening, there can be no learning.

Students come in many mannerisms: meek and lowly, and bold, strong and weak. The bold and strong students should not bully the weak ones.

There is a saying that empty vessels make the most noise. The student that is quiet listens, and when one listens-he or she hears and learns.

The student that talks all the time is, noisy and cannot hear the teacher and other students. Therefore, he misses a lot from too much noise making. I believe our young people are very wise people and a word is enough for the wise."

At this time Mr. Blake took the microphone and called on the neighborhood musicians who sang a rap song and as usual the hall was bursting with students dancing to the music and having fun. The students danced themselves to exhaustion.

The Symposium teaches on America the Unique Society.

Mr. Blake now called Ms. Laura. Ms. Laura talked about America the Unique Society. She came and said, "thank you wonderful audience. You have been awesome today. America is one of the most unique societies where students go to school free from elementary to high school. In college, all you need to do is to be in good standing academically to qualify for a loan. The children have access to good education whether from rich or poor parents. We can only show appreciation by handling school property with care." Five students came to show how books and test tubes should be handled. Jessy mistakenly dropped the test tube in an effort to do a good job. She was very repentant as she ran after the tube and picked it up where it rolled to. This is the kind of attitude you need in handling school property properly. Books should not be torn up. There are societies where poor children cannot get an education. Only the 'haves', not the 'have-nots', can go to school. There are countries like that, but we are blessed in the USA, where schools and books are free up to high school."

Princess James gave a vote of thanks. "Thank you, wonderful people. You have been great today! We thank God for this special and eventful day. We have heard that the school premises should be kept sacred, and there should be no surprises of any sort on school grounds, and in appearance students should be properly and neatly dressed.

"A classroom should be calm and peaceful for learning. The teacher or any adult in the classroom must be duly respected. Students should respect each other, and be each other's keepers or care for each other. School property must also be preserved—God bless you all."

The crowd cheered. Mr. George came up to Mrs. James and said, "Some young people are raising their hands over there." "Do you have any questions," Mrs. James said? "When is the next symposium?," the student asked. "Alright," said Mrs. James, "It seems like this will be a quarterly affair. You will be notified." Good night and God bless you all."

The kids trooped out joyfully. Morris and his friends headed home with others.

"I wish there will be another symposium tomorrow." "I do too," John added. It is really cool. Thanks for inviting us." Nancy, John's sister said to Morris, "that was fun; you get a hug for taking us to the symposium." Nancy hugged Morris and he blushed. That sweet hug lingered in his mind all night long. John thought-this is a day to remember. I think I like Nancy.

www.ingramcontent.com/pod-product-compliance
Lightning Source LLC
Chambersburg PA
CBHW070454170726
48291CB00005B/1757

* 9 7 8 1 9 4 9 7 4 6 0 6 8 *